This book belongs to

....

This is the story of Goldilocks,

a little girl who never knocks.

And on every page, there's

a clock to spot!

Goldilocks
and the
Three Bears

Illustrations by Sara Baker

make
believe
ideas

The three bears are hungry.
Their breakfast is ready.
But the porridge is too hot.

8

So Daddy Bear, Mommy Bear,
and Baby Bear go for a walk.

Who is this?
It is Goldilocks!
She runs into the house.

Daddy Bear's porridge is too hot.
Mommy Bear's porridge is too cold.
Baby Bear's porridge is just right.
Goldilocks eats it all up!

Daddy Bear's chair is too hard.
Mommy Bear's chair is too soft.
Baby Bear's chair is just right.
But it breaks!

Daddy Bear's bed is too high.
Mommy Bear's bed is too low.
Baby Bear's bed is just right.

"Someone has eaten my porridge!" cries Baby Bear.

"Someone has
broken my chair!"
cries Baby Bear.

"Someone is sleeping
in my bed!" cries Baby Bear.
Goldilocks wakes up.

Goldilocks runs away
as fast as she can!

Ready to tell

Oh no! Some of the pictures from this story have gotten mixed up! Can you retell the story and point to each picture in the correct order?

Picture dictionary

Encourage your child to read these words from the story and gradually develop his or her basic vocabulary.

bear

bed

breakfast

broken

chair

hot

porridge

sleeping

walk

I • up • look • we • like • and • on • at • for •

Key words

Here are some key words used in context. Help your child to use other words from the border in simple sentences.

Breakfast **is** ready.

Goldilocks eats **the** porridge.

She breaks the chair.

She sleeps **in** the bed.

Goldilocks runs **away**.

a • he • is • said • go • you • are • this • going • they • away • play • cat • to

am • can • yes • It • see • she • me • or • was • went • In • come • get • day

the • dog • big • my • mom • no • dad • all •

Make yummy porridge!

Goldilocks loved the three bears' porridge.
Try making some yourself from this delicious
traditional porridge recipe from Scotland.

You will need
- 1 cup oatmeal • 4 cups cold water • $1/2$ tsp salt
- 2 tsp sugar • $1/2$ cup buttermilk or cream

What to do
1 Put the oatmeal into a saucepan with the cold water.
2 Stir gently over a medium heat until the mixture
starts to boil.
3 Lower the heat and continue to stir – to avoid any
lumps – for five minutes. The mixture will become thick
and creamy.
4 Add the salt, sugar, and buttermilk or cream.
5 Give the porridge a final stir and serve hot.

Porridge tastes great with:
- raspberries
- maple syrup and whipped cream
- chocolate raisins
- raisins and cinnamon
- applesauce and cinnamon
- sliced bananas